The Tidy Fairy

Copyright © QED Publishing 2005

First published in the UK in 2005 by
QED Publishing
A Quarto Group company
226 City Road
London EC1V 2TT
www.qed-publishing.co.uk

A Catalogue record for this book is available from the British Library.

ISBN 1 84538 154 8

Written by Sally Hewitt
Designed by Caroline Grimshaw
Editor Hannah Ray
Illustrated by Jacqueline East

Series Consultant Anne Faundez
Publisher Steve Evans
Creative Director Louise Morley
Editorial Manager Jean Coppendale

Printed and bound in China

The Tidy Fairy

Sally Hewitt

QED Publishing

Every night, Tina and Bertie climb into their bunk beds.

Sometimes Bertie wants Tina's top bunk and they have a pillow fight.

4

Every morning, Mum shouts, "You'll be late for school!" – so they get dressed and race downstairs.

Every day, while Tina and Bertie are at school, the Tidy Fairy makes their beds, folds their clothes and puts their toys away in the toy box.

Every afternoon, when they get back from school,
Tina and Bertie make their room untidy all over again.

Today, Mum has a phone call from Granny.
She looks worried.

"Granny has hurt her leg," Mum says.
"I must go and look after her."

"But who will look after us?" wail Tina and Bertie.

"I'll ask Auntie Jo," says Mum.

Tina and Bertie love Auntie Jo. She takes
them to the park and buys them treats.
She has never been to stay before.

When Auntie Jo arrives, they all wave goodbye to Mum.

"Send our love to Granny," they say.

"Be good!" says Mum.

11

Tina and Bertie play in their bedroom while Auntie Jo cooks supper.

Bertie ruins Tina's jigsaw puzzle, so Tina knocks over Bertie's bricks.

12

Auntie Jo calls, "Supper's ready!" and
Tina and Bertie race downstairs.

13

At bedtime, Auntie Jo comes into
the bedroom to say goodnight.
"What a mess!" she says. "Who's going
to tidy this up? The Tidy Fairy?"

Tina and Bertie giggle.

In the morning, Tina and Bertie go to school.

When they get home, their bedroom is still a mess!

"The Tidy Fairy didn't come today," says Auntie Jo.
"You'll have to tidy your bedroom yourselves."

The Tidy Fairy doesn't come the next day or the day after that!

Tina and Bertie have to keep tidying their bedroom themselves.

When Mum comes back from Granny's house, Tina and Bertie ask, "When is the Tidy Fairy coming back? We've had to tidy our bedroom ourselves!"

"Now she knows you're so good at tidying, she won't come back," says Mum.

"Oh no!" say Tina and Bertie.

Mum gives Auntie Jo a big wink!

What do you think?

Why do Tina and Bertie have a pillow fight?

What toys do Tina and Bertie make a mess with in their bedroom?

Look at page 6. Why is the bedroom tidy when Tina and Bertie get home?

Why does the phone call make Mum look worried?

Look at page 9. Why are Tina and Bertie worried?

Why is the bedroom still a mess when Tina and Bertie get back from school on page 15?

Is there really a Tidy Fairy?

Why does Mum give
Auntie Jo a big wink?

Parents' and teachers' notes

- Look at the cover together and talk about the picture. Can your child describe the cover? What can he or she see?
- Read the title and explain that the title is the name of the story.
- Look through the book, concentrating on the illustrations. Discuss how the story is told by the illustrations, as well as by the words.
- Read the story together and then discuss what the story is about. Ask your child to re-tell the story to you, in his or her own words.
- Explain to your child that this story is about children of a similar age to him or her. Talk about whether what happens in the story could happen to your child or to his or her friends.
- Talk about how Tina and Bertie learn a lesson in the story (i.e. that their mess doesn't get tidied up by magic, someone has to do it).

- Talk about how Mum learns a lesson in the story, too (i.e. that if she always tidies up after Tina and Bertie, then they will never do it for themselves).
- Discuss what Auntie Jo did to get the children to tidy their bedroom. (She didn't tidy up and told Tina and Bertie that the Tidy Fairy hadn't come, so they had to tidy up themselves.)
- Talk about how magic doesn't really happen in this story. Think of some stories you have read together in which magic does happen.
- Together, make a list of things that your child can do to help at home. Talk about which jobs your child enjoys doing, and which he or she doesn't enjoy.
- Help your child to make up a story about himself or herself. Write the story for your child and encourage him or her to draw some illustrations to accompany the text.